Sherlock Holmes
The Man with the Twisted Lip

ReadZone Books Limited

© 2015 ReadZone Books Limited

This edition is an easy-to-read adaptation of *The Man with the Twisted Lip* by Arthur Conan Doyle, which was first published by Strand Magazine in 1891.

Originally published in the Netherlands as *De man met het litteken*
© 2014 Uitgeverij Eenvoudig Communiceren, Amsterdam

Copyright © Helene Bakker 2014
Translation: Anna Asbury
Design: Nicolet Oost Lievense
Cover design: Jurian Wiese
Images: Shutterstock

Printed in Malta by Melita Press

British Library Cataloguing in Publication Data (CIP) is available for this title.

ISBN 978 1 78322 538 5

Visit our website: www.readzonebooks.com

Sherlock Holmes
The Man with the Twisted Lip

The famous story by Arthur Conan Doyle,
retold by Helene Bakker

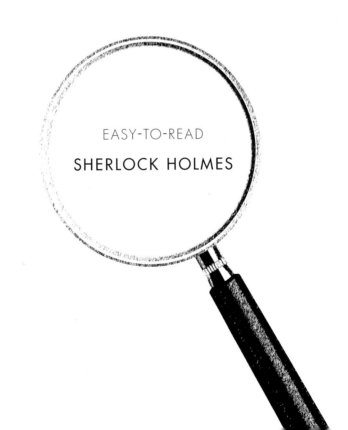

EASY-TO-READ

SHERLOCK HOLMES

Sherlock Holmes was a famous English private detective. He didn't really exist, but the writer Arthur Conan Doyle wrote so well that many people think he did.

Sherlock Holmes started work as a detective about 150 years ago in the city of London, along with his friend Doctor Watson. The way Holmes solved attacks and murders has made him famous all over the world. Even today, films are still made about his detective work.

CHAPTER 1
Opium

Opium is a drug you can become addicted to. In Sherlock Holmes's time, opium was sold in opium dens. These were dark cellars where addicts could lie and smoke opium pipes.

Watson, Sherlock Holmes's friend, no longer lived with Holmes. Watson was married and had become a family doctor. His practice was in a different neighbourhood.

A couple of his patients were drug addicts.

One of them was Isa Whitney.

Isa had once been a strong lad.

He was cheerful and ready to help anyone. He was married to a lovely woman.

When he started smoking opium, though, things went wrong. He changed into a poor wretch. Opium – that's all his life revolved around.

It was because of this man Isa Whitney that Watson ended up in an opium den.

This is what happened....

CHAPTER 2
Isa Whitney

Watson and his wife have just finished dinner when the doorbell rings. Kate, Isa Whitney's wife, is standing on the doorstep.

Watson sees her, and knows immediately what the problem is. She looks so anxious.

'Is there something wrong with Isa?' he says.

Yes, she nods, and the tears stream down her cheeks.

'Come on in and have a good cry. You'll soon feel better.'

'Oh, Doctor,' says the woman when she's a bit calmer, 'I'm so afraid. You know Isa well, don't you?'

'Yes, he's been coming here a long time.'

'You know he's an addict, don't you?'

'Yes, I know.'

'Yesterday he left very early, around seven o'clock.

To go to one of those dreadful opium dens. I begged him not to go. I tried everything. But he said he had to go.

'I don't understand it, Doctor. He's such a lovely man, but that dreadful opium...'

She starts crying again.

'It's not your fault. Really, there's nothing you can do about it,' Watson comforts her.

His words seem to help a bit. She calms down.

'Tell me more, Kate.'

She nods and continues hesitantly.

'Isa isn't home yet, Doctor. He's already been away two days and a night. Something must have happened. He's never stayed away so long before.'

'Well, two days in an opium den is a long time.'

'And do you know the worst of it, Doctor?'

'No.'

'I daren't go looking for him. I daren't go into one of those dens.'

Suddenly Watson understands why Kate has come.

'Would you like me to come with you to look?' he asks.

'Oh, please, if you would, Doctor!'

'Do you know where he went?'

'No, only that he's on the east side of town.'

Watson thinks for a moment. The east side of town... there is an opium den there... the Bar of Gold or something.

But the poor woman can't go along to such a dark, dangerous cellar!

So he says, 'Kate, how about this? You just stay here with my wife. I'll go in search of Isa alone. I think I know where he's gone. If he's still there, we'll be back here together within two hours.'

So Watson leaves in search of Isa Whitney.

CHAPTER 3
In the opium den

The driver of the carriage knows the way to the Bar of Gold.

'Near the port, Doctor. It's a bad neighbourhood. I don't like going there. I hope I can get my carriage through those narrow streets. It's so dark there too, but I'll do it for you.'

Luckily their journey goes smoothly. The carriage stops in a narrow alley.

Watson sees steps leading down to a cellar.

A lamp burns above the cellar door.

On a wooden board under the lamp he reads the words 'Bar of Gold'.

'Take care, Doctor,' says the driver as Watson steps out.

'Yes, I will,' says Watson as calmly as he can, but his heart is thumping.

'Just stay here and wait for me, driver. I'll be

back within half an hour.'

'Still alive, I hope,' the man grumbles.

A moment later Watson is standing in a long, low room with wooden benches on either side.

The air is heavy with opium smoke. Through it he can dimly see some people lying on the benches.

Here and there small red flames flare up, one moment bright, then dim again.

Those must be the pipe heads with the poisonous opium in them, he thinks.

He hesitates a moment. Should he just walk on through?

A waiter is already approaching him.

The waiter has an opium pipe ready and is about to lead him to an empty bench.

'No, thank you,' says Watson.

'I don't want to stay. There's a friend of mine here. I'd like to speak to him for a moment. His name is Isa Whitney.'

There is a cry from the right-hand side. Something moves.

Watson peers into the darkness and suddenly he sees Isa lying there. Isa, who looks at him wildly.

'My God, it's the doctor!' Isa cries out.

Watson walks towards him.

Only now does he see how bad Isa looks.

'What's the time?' asks Isa.

'Nine o'clock in the evening.'

'And what day is it?'

'Friday.'

'What? Friday! That can't be right. It's Wednesday, isn't it? It must be Wednesday! Why are you trying to scare me?'

'It really is Friday, man. Your wife has been waiting for you for two days. You should be ashamed.'

'I am, but how can it be Friday?' Isa moans.

'I've only been here a couple of hours. Three or four pipes...'

'Oh, Isa, don't talk nonsense. It really is Friday. Just come with me now. Your wife's waiting for you.'

'Yes, I'm coming. I mustn't keep dear Kate

waiting any longer. But, please help me stand up. I feel so weak.'

Watson lifts Isa up.

He quickly gives Isa his arm to stop him from falling.

'I still have to pay, Doctor, but I feel so strange. Would you do it? The money's in my pocket.'

'All right,' says Watson.

He looks around for the waiter, but no one comes forward.

Slowly the two men shuffle towards the door.

It's not easy, as Isa is leaning heavily on Watson and there is little room between the benches.

Suddenly someone tugs at Watson's jacket.

He hears someone say, 'Walk past me, then look round.'

He hears this loud and clear.

Watson looks down. There is a man by the walkway, dazed from the opium.

He looks asleep.

An opium pipe swings softly back and forth.

This must be the man who spoke to him.

Watson doesn't know what's going on.

He takes another two steps and looks round.

Just in time, Watson holds back a cry of surprise.

The man grinning at Watson's surprise is none other than... Sherlock Holmes.

CHAPTER 4
Sherlock Holmes

Watson bends down.

'Holmes,' he whispers, 'What are you doing in this den?'

'Speak more quietly,' Holmes mumbles in his role as an addict.

'I want to talk to you for a moment,' he mumbles on.

'Send that friend of yours on home.'

'I can't let him go alone, can I? Anyway, there's a carriage waiting for me outside.'

'That's perfect. Then send him home in it. That man's so dim-witted, he won't even notice he's alone. Do it for me.'

'Well, all right then,' says Watson quietly.

'Give the driver a note for your wife, Watson.

Tell her you'll be away a while because you've run into me.'

Watson nods.

'Go on,' whispers Holmes.

'Wait for me outside. I'll be with you in five minutes.'

Surprised, Watson shuffles onwards with Isa, who hasn't noticed much of the conversation with Holmes, or at least he doesn't mention it.

When they're nearing the way out, the waiter comes over.

Watson pays and leaves the cellar with Isa.

The driver is glad to see Watson again.

'Thank God, Doctor, you're still alive!' he calls out.

'Yes, I found what I was looking for. Isa, in you get!'

He pushes Isa into the carriage.

It's quite awkward.

When he finally gets him on to the bench, Isa falls off. He's asleep.

Watson pulls a piece of notepaper from his pocket and starts writing.

Suddenly he feels the carriage start moving.

'Wait, wait! Stop!' he cries to the front. 'I'm not coming with you!'

The driver hears him. He stops the horse and looks around in surprise.

'I'm staying here,' says Watson.

'Here?' the driver shouts.

'Yes, here. Take this man to our house and give my wife this note.'

'But I can't leave you alone here, can I?'

'Just do as I say, my dear man. I'll be fine. When my wife reads this note, she'll understand everything.'

'Well, as you wish, Doctor, but I think it's dangerous. Take good care of yourself.'

'And you take good care of Isa Whitney. He must reach home safe and sound,' says Watson.

What a mess Isa has made of his life, thinks Watson, as the carriage moves out of the alley.

But where has Sherlock Holmes got to?

CHAPTER 5
Neville's gone

At last the door of the opium den opens. A man stumbles out. His back is bent over. Watson walks behind him out of the alley and into another.

Then the man bursts out laughing and stands up straight.

'Watson! Fancy running into you in that hole. You didn't think I'd taken to opium, did you?'

Now Watson laughs.

'I was just very surprised, Holmes.'

'I was too. What were you doing there?'

'I was looking for a patient of mine.'

'I was looking for an enemy.'

'An enemy?'

'Yes. I wanted to find out something in that opium den. They're a gang of scoundrels in there. Terrible.'

'Are they? I thought they were poor miserable creatures.'

'Don't let them fool you, Watson. Did you know at the back of that cellar there's a hatch that opens out right onto the river?

'And do you know that sometimes someone is tied up and pushed through it?'

'No, really? That's murder!'

'Precisely! And the owner of that cellar is the biggest scoundrel. I was sitting near him. I hoped to learn something from what he said from time to time.'

'Well, did you hear anything?'

'No, nothing,' Holmes sighs.

'Who are you looking for then?' Watson asks curiously.

'A young businessman. Neville St. Clair is his name. He vanished without a trace on Monday. The police have searched the whole neighbourhood, but they haven't found him.'

CHAPTER 6
A box of bricks

Holmes lights his pipe and draws on it deeply a couple of times.

'So now you're investigating the case further, are you?' asks Watson.

'Yes, and I need you for that. Listen carefully. I want you to keep a lookout on the stairs in a moment. Then I can go and take a look in the rooms above the opium den.'

'Above the opium den? Why?'

'Because Neville St. Clair was last seen there,' says Holmes.

'His own wife saw him standing at the window there on Monday.'

'She was walking along the alley on her way to the station when she suddenly heard a scream. She was startled, because she recognised the voice... It was her husband's. She looked up and saw him standing above the Bar of Gold.

'It had to be him. She can't have been mistaken, as she could clearly see his face. He saw her too. He waved his arms wildly in the air… and suddenly he was gone, as if someone pulled him back quickly.'

'Did she see anyone else?'

'No, no one else. And do you know the strange thing? Neville St. Clair was only wearing a coat, with nothing underneath! No shirt, no tie… he was naked.'

'Of course she was very shocked and wanted to go to him, but when she tried to go up the stairs, the owner of the opium den stopped her. He wouldn't let her up.

'She ran out of the alley in a panic. Around the corner she almost ran right into two policemen. She quickly told them what had happened and the two immediately went back to the house with her.

'The owner was still standing at the bottom of the stairs. "This is my house", he screamed. "You have no business here."

'But the police took no notice of him.

They entered the room where the woman had seen her husband, but the room was empty. Not a trace of Neville St. Clair.

'The other rooms on that floor were also empty, apart from a small side room. There was a crippled old man on the floor, a beggar.

'The police knew him, as he had been begging in this neighbourhood for years. He rented the little room. "I didn't see or hear anyone", he said, when one of the policemen asked about Neville St. Clair.

'The police decided to give up their investigation. They told Mrs St. Clair that she must have dreamt it.

'They had barely said this when the woman gave a cry and snatched up a small wooden box. She pulled at the lid and a set of bricks rolled onto the floor.

'In tears, she told them that her husband had promised to give the box of bricks to their little son. He had been planning to do so that very evening.

'The police then understood that something must have happened. "We'll search all the rooms again", they said, "But really carefully this time"'.

'They didn't find anything, did they, Holmes?' Watson asks.

'Well, I can't say that. They found clothes belonging to Neville St. Clair and traces of blood in a wardrobe in the beggar's room.'

'Blood?'

'Yes, there was some blood on the floor and the window frame, but Neville St. Clair himself had disappeared.'

'The River Thames runs behind the house, doesn't it? Maybe they pushed him through an open window and he drowned.'

Watson looks at Holmes.

'Maybe,' says Holmes, drawing on his pipe again.

Slowly Holmes and Watson walk back to the opium den.

'What do you actually plan to do up there?' asks Watson when they come to the door.

'Take a look and see if there's another way out. There might well be a secret stairway at the back.'

'But what about that beggar? He lives there, doesn't he? Won't he be at home?'

'No. They took him to the police station on Monday. He's still locked up, but I'll tell you more about that later. First I want to go inside. Come with me.'

CHAPTER 7

Above the Bar of Gold

Sherlock Holmes picks the lock with a short piece of wire, and very softly Watson and he climb up to the floor above the Bar of Gold.

'You keep watch here, Watson,' says Holmes.

'Warn me if you hear anyone downstairs go outside, because we should turn the light off then.'

'All right,' says Watson. He sits at the top of the steps. Holmes goes into one of the back rooms.

His lantern swings back and forth. Long shadows dance against the wall.

Suddenly Watson hears a door open.

'Holmes,' he hisses, 'Put the lamp out! Someone's coming out.'

Sherlock immediately puts the lamp out. He comes out of the backroom in darkness.

'Stay here, Watson,' he whispers. 'I'm going to the front room.'

Carefully Holmes opens the door of the front room.

The moonlight shines in.

He goes to stand by the window. He looks out, motionless... one minute... two minutes... five minutes.

Then Holmes relights the lamp.

He looks around a bit in the front room and comes back.

'We're leaving, Watson. I've seen enough here. There's nothing to be found.'

CHAPTER 8
On the way to Lee

'Watson, are you coming to Lee?' asks Holmes when they're outside. 'Madam is very kind and there are two beds in my room.'

'Lee – where's that? And who's Madam?', Watson asks in surprise.

'Mrs St. Clair. She lives in Lee, ten kilometres from here. I'm staying there while this investigation goes on. She'll be fine with you coming along. You'd like to come, wouldn't you?'

'Yes, I don't feel like going home now. It's late and my wife knows I'm with you.'

'Good. Look, we're in luck. There's a carriage.'

Holmes points to a carriage. The driver is waiting for a new customer to come along.

Holmes and Watson climb in quickly and ask to go to Lee.

For a while Holmes says nothing. He lights his pipe and thinks deeply.

They're already outside London when he looks

up and says he can't work it out.

He doesn't understand what Neville St. Clair was doing in that house, nor why his clothes were there.

'That beggar,' says Watson. 'You were going to tell me something about that beggar.'

'Oh, yes, the crippled beggar. Hugh Boone is his name. Everyone in the neighbourhood knows him. He's in the same spot every day, legs crossed and his hat on the ground in front of him. That's how he earns his money.

'If you walk past him, you can't help seeing him. He stands out with his red hair, and there's a big brown scar running from his upper lip to his ear. His mouth is completely twisted out of shape by it.

'He can't walk, but he can talk. He's always telling jokes, so everyone likes him. All the same, I don't trust him, Watson. He says he didn't hear or see Neville St. Clair, but he's lying. He must have something to do with him.'

'You don't mean he did something to Neville St. Clair, do you?'

'Perhaps.'

'A crippled old man against a strong young fellow?'

'He only has trouble walking. You know how it is, Watson. If you can't use your legs, you have to do everything with your arms. That old man may have very strong arms.'

'Yes, that's possible.'

'I told you they found blood too, didn't I?'

'Yes.'

'The beggar told the police it was his blood. He said he'd cut his finger. He did have a big cut, one of the policemen told me, so that might be true, but he's lying about Neville St. Clair's clothes,' says Holmes with a sigh. 'They were in his wardrobe. He must have seen them. Do you believe he wouldn't know what was in his own wardrobe?'

'No, not really.'

'Well, nor me.'

Holmes draws on his pipe again and says, 'Have I told you yet what they found in the river?'

'No.'

'The police searched the river for Neville St. Clair's body. They didn't find it, but his coat was found in the mud, and what do you think they found in his coat pockets?'

'I have no idea.'

'All his pockets were full of coins. There were more than six hundred altogether.'

Watson looks at his friend in surprise.

'More than six hundred?'

'Yes. His coat sank like a stone with all that money.'

'Holmes, I'm starting to understand!' Watson cries out excitedly.

'What are you starting to understand?' Holmes asks curiously.

'Well, only a beggar would have so many coins. The beggar must have filled his pockets, mustn't he?'

'Good thinking, Watson.'

'And I suspect,' Watson continues, 'That he also planned on throwing away the other clothes, but didn't have time. He must have heard the police coming upstairs, so then he quickly hid them in his wardrobe.'

Holmes nods. 'That'll be it, but I still don't understand what Neville was doing in that house.'

Holmes stares outside with a gloomy face. Suddenly the carriage stops.

'Here we are, Watson. This is Neville St. Clair's house.'

CHAPTER 9
A letter

'Well?' shouts a voice as Holmes and Watson step out of the carriage.

A small, dark haired woman runs up to them.

'Is there any news yet?'

Holmes shakes his head.

'No good news?'

'No.'

'No bad news either?'

'No.'

'Good, at least there's still hope, then,' she says.

Holmes sees that the woman is looking at Watson. 'This is my friend, Doctor Watson. He often helps me. You don't mind him coming along, do you?'

'Of course not,' she says in a friendly voice.

'The more people looking for Neville, the better!'

'Do you mind if he stays the night? There are two beds in my room.'

'No, that's fine. Come on in.'

They walk into a magnificent house.

'I've made soup. I thought you might like some.'

Holmes and Watson nod.

After the soup Mrs St. Clair sits opposite Holmes.

'I want to ask you something,' she says. She looks at him intently. 'And I want a very honest answer.'

'Ask away.'

'Do you think my husband is still alive?'

Holmes hesitates. He clearly finds it a difficult question.

'Be honest,' she repeats.

'I... eh... I don't really think so.'

'You think he's dead?'

'He might be.'

'And what day did he die?'

'Monday.'

'That can't be right, Mr Holmes. I received a letter from him this morning.'

'What?' Holmes cries out.

'Yes, this morning!' She waves a letter in the air.

'May I?' Holmes asks.

'Yes, of course. Go ahead and read it.'

Watson has gone to stand behind Holmes and looks over his shoulder as he reads.

Holmes points to the envelope. It's addressed to:

> *Mrs St. Clair*
> *The Cedars*
> *Lee*

'Is this written by your husband?' he asks.

'No, that's not his handwriting, but there's a note inside, and he did write that.'

Holmes stares at the address.

'Strange,' he says. 'Do you see that the name has been written with a different pen from the address?'

'Oh yes.' Watson now sees it too.

'The name is in a lighter colour.'

'Right. That might be very important.'

'Why?' asks Mrs St. Clair in surprise.

'Because it means that the writer didn't know your address. First he wrote your name and only later the address. So he didn't know you and your husband very well.'

'Well, I see what you mean now.'

'Now for the letter.'

Holmes pulls a small sheet of paper out of the envelope. On it is written in pencil:

> *Darling,*
> *Don't be afraid. It's a mistake.*
> *Everything will be fine.*
> *It just might take a little while.*
> *Neville*

'Did your husband write this?' he asks.

'Yes, and there was something else in the letter. Look, this!'

She shows them a signet ring hanging on a chain around her neck.

'This is his signet ring.'

'Well,' says Holmes, 'Then your husband must have written this letter. But that envelope...'

He takes another close look at it.

'Perhaps your husband wrote the letter on Monday, and perhaps someone else wrote on the envelope later. That would mean...'

'Oh, no,' Mrs St. Clair cries out.

'That can't be true. I don't believe you.'

She starts to cry.

Holmes tries to comfort her.

'Perhaps you're right, Mrs St. Clair. Perhaps your husband is still alive. That letter has at least given me some hope.'

'Good,' says the woman with a deep sigh, wiping away her tears.

'I thought you were going to give up on the case,' she says shortly afterwards.

'Give up? In the middle of an investigation? No, Mrs St. Clair, you don't know me at all. Sherlock Holmes finishes what he starts.'

She looks at him gratefully.

'Try to get some sleep now,' says Holmes.

'Tomorrow I'll continue searching for your husband, along with Watson.

'One more thing. Have you ever noticed your husband using opium?'

'No, never.'

'Good. Then it's time we went to our room, don't you think, Watson?'

Watson nods. He's very tired.

CHAPTER 10
Holmes thinks

Watson goes straight to bed.

Holmes doesn't.

He can never sleep when he's working on a difficult case.

At night he stays up thinking for as long as it takes to find a solution.

Tonight Sherlock stays up.

He's taken his coat and waistcoat off and put on a long dressing gown.

He's sitting on the floor, legs crossed, a pipe in his mouth and a jar of tobacco in front of him.

Watson sees him sitting like that just before he falls asleep.

He sees him still sitting like that when he wakes up hours later, but now Holmes isn't looking so gloomy.

Watson sees his eyes sparkling.

'Are you awake, Watson?'

'Yes.'

'Feel like a morning drive?'

'Fine with me.'

'Good. Get dressed. Then we'll get going before Mrs St. Clair wakes up. I've already seen someone walking towards the stable. I'll go and ask if he can take us to London in the carriage.'

Holmes stands up. He takes off his dressing gown, puts on his waistcoat and overcoat, and leaves the room.

Watson quickly gets dressed. He's curious. What could Holmes have come up with? Why's he in such a hurry? And why does he want to leave so early? It's only six o'clock.

He's just dressed when Holmes returns.

'We can leave. The stable boy will take us.'

'I'm ready,' says Watson. 'I'm waiting for you now.'

He looks at Holmes.

Holmes gets his things together, puts them in his bag, and says mysteriously, 'I think I know it, Watson.'

'What do you know?'

'The key to the case.'

'I'm curious.'

'The key comes from the bathroom.'

'The bathroom?' Watson looks at his friend in surprise.

'Yes, and it's no joke. I've just been there and I've put the key in my bag.'

Watson continues to stare at him, surprised.

'Come on, Watson. We're leaving now. I'm not telling you anything. You'll soon see what I mean.'

Laughing and swinging his bag, Holmes walks out in front of Watson to the carriage.

CHAPTER 11
The man with the twisted lip

It's about seven o'clock when they drive into London. They cross the Thames and drive in the direction of the docks to the east.

'Are we going back to that opium den?' Watson wants to know.

'No, we're going to the police station where that beggar is locked up.'

Holmes gives the driver some directions and soon they're there.

'Shall I wait?' asks the driver.

'No, you go on home, and tell Mrs St. Clair where we are.'

The two policemen standing at the desk greet Holmes politely.

They already know him.

'Who's on duty?' asks Holmes.

'Inspector Bradstreet, sir.'

'Good. I know him.'

Holmes and Watson walk through.

There's an office at the start of a flagstone passage.

Holmes knocks on the door.

A big, fat man opens up.

'Sherlock Holmes! What are you doing here?' he cries out, surprised.

The two men shake hands warmly.

'This is Watson, my friend.'

'Come on in. Tell me what I can do for you,' says the inspector.

They walk into the office and sit down.

Inspector Bradstreet looks at Holmes questioningly.

'Tell all, Holmes. I'm curious what you're up to these days.'

'I'm here for Boone, the crippled beggar. He's here, isn't he?' Holmes asks.

'Oh, him! He's here in connection with the disappearance of Neville St. Clair.'

'That's the one. How are things with him?'

'We haven't had any trouble with him. He's kept calm, but he's a dirty fellow.'

'Dirty?'

'Yes, he's as filthy as anything. He refuses to wash, whatever we try, and he won't put clean clothes on either.'

A smile appears on Holmes's face.

'Aha… that's lucky,' he says mysteriously. 'I would very much like to see him.'

'Fine, come along with me. You can leave your bag here.'

'No, I'll bring it, thanks.'

They walk along the flagstone passage to a door with a big padlock.

'The prison,' says Inspector Bradstreet, as he opens the door.

They enter another passage. 'Third door on the right,' says Bradstreet. 'Here, this one!'

He opens a small hatch in the upper part of the door and looks in.

'He's asleep,' he whispers. 'Look.'

One by one Holmes and Watson look through the hatch.

The beggar is lying with his face towards them. He's snoring.

He's still wearing his coat, all old and torn and stained.

His face and hands are really dirty, but under the dirt they can clearly see the dark scar. It twists his lips apart, as if he's grinning.

His red hair falls over his eyes.

'Handsome fellow, isn't he?' the inspector says quietly.

'Time he had a wash,' Holmes remarks.

'Luckily I planned for that. I've brought something with me...'

Watson and Bradstreet look at Holmes in surprise.

He opens his bag and takes out a big sponge.

'Pay attention,' he says next.

'Bradstreet, if you open the door quietly, I'll take care of the rest.'

The inspector carefully puts the key in the lock and opens the door.

Holmes enters the cell walking on tiptoe.

The beggar continues to sleep.

Holmes bends down over a bowl of water and dips the sponge in.

Then he wipes the wet sponge a couple of times firmly over the beggar Hugh Boone's face.

'May I introduce you to Neville St. Clair!' he calls out.

Then in one tug he pulls away the shock of red hair.

On the bed lies a pale man with black hair.

The scar is gone!

The twisted lip is gone!

Sleepily he sits up and looks around. Then he suddenly realises what has happened. With a scream he falls back and buries his face in the pillow.

'Heavens above!' cries the inspector.

'It's him! It's Neville St. Clair, the man we're looking for! I recognise him.'

The man sits up again and looks at the inspector.

'If that's true, if I'm Neville St. Clair,' he says, 'Why am I locked up in here?'

'For the murder of Neville St... Wait a minute... That can't be right! It must be suicide,' says the inspector, grinning.

'I haven't committed any crime,' says Neville.

Holmes looks at him angrily.

'No, not a crime, but you're a cheat. You never told anyone what you were doing during the day. Even your wife doesn't know.'

'No, of course not! If she knew... Oh, what a scandal, how terrible... She mustn't find out. What can I do?'

He covers his face with his hands in desperation.

Holmes sits down next to him on the bed.

'Listen carefully, Neville. You have two choices: you can keep quiet, or you can tell us everything. If you keep quiet, you'll have to tell the whole story in court, and you know that means it'll all come out in the newspapers?'

'Oh God, how terrible. I'd rather die!'

'Or you can tell us everything now,' Holmes continues.

'If you can convince us that you haven't done anything wrong, the case will never go to court. No one else will know anything about it.'

'Is that possible?' asks Neville, relieved.

'Yes, it is, but you have to tell us everything honestly.'

'All right, I'll do that.'

'Fire away, then,' says Holmes.

Watson has also sat down on the bed, and Inspector Bradstreet sits on a stool directly in front of Neville.

They listen.

CHAPTER 12
Explanation

'I used to work for a newspaper,' Neville St. Clair begins.

'One day I had to write a piece about beggars in London. In order to find out as much as possible, I decided to become a beggar for a while myself.

'I painted my face with a big scar. Using a small strip of plaster, I pulled one side of my upper lip upwards. Add to that a red wig and old clothes, and I was ready.

'I started to limp and became Boone the miserable beggar.

'The first day I sat in a busy spot for seven hours. When I got home in the evening, my pockets were full of coins. I counted them up. To my surprise, I had made good money that day, as much as I would normally earn in a week.

'The following day I sat in the street again,

and the day after too.

'The money kept on coming in. You probably already get it. I gave up my job and became a beggar. With some face paint, old clothes and a hat, sitting on the ground, I became rich.'

'When did you start?' asks Holmes.

'Seven years ago.'

'And no one knows?'

'Only one man, the owner of the Bar of Gold. He knows. I've been renting a room above his opium den for seven years. That's where I get changed, and sometimes I sleep there.

'I pay that man well, because I want to be sure he'll keep my secret.

'I grew richer and richer, and I bought a house outside the city. That's where I met my wife. She thinks she's married to a businessman, but I've never told her what kind of business I do.'

'And on Monday, what happened then? Your wife saw you, is that it?'

'Yes, I had just finished work...'

Inspector Bradstreet sneers. 'Begging, do you call that work?'

Neville blushes. He hesitates.

'Go on. What happened?' asks Holmes.

'I... eh.... I was in my room. As I was changing my clothes, I looked out of the window, and suddenly I saw my wife. She was standing in the street and looking right at me. It was a terrible shock.

'I buried my face in my hands and ran from the window. I screamed to the bar owner that he was not to let anyone come upstairs.

'A little later I heard my wife talking to him downstairs. I was afraid she would come up, so I quickly put my beggar's clothes back on and put some face paint on.

'Then I realised the room might be searched, and that my wife would recognise my clothes. So I grabbed my good coat, where I had just put all the money from that day. I ran to the window at the back of the house and threw it into the river. In my hurry to open the window, I cut myself.

'I wanted to throw my other clothes out too, but by then the police had arrived. You know the rest. I was arrested, suspected of the murder of Neville St. Clair.'

There is silence for a moment.

'That letter,' says Holmes. 'When did you write that letter to your wife?'

'On Monday, when everyone was searching the other rooms. I gave my letter and my ring to the bar owner. If I were caught, he was to send it to my wife immediately.'

'He did that, but not immediately. She only received it yesterday morning.'

'Oh, no! She must have been so worried.'

'Yes,' nods Holmes, 'and that's why she called me in.'

'Neville St. Clair,' says Inspector Bradstreet very solemnly, 'Can we trust that Hugh Boone the beggar no longer exists?'

'Yes, Inspector, I promise,' replies Neville firmly.

'Good, then we'll forget the case. You can go home.'

'Thank you.'

'You needn't thank me. Sherlock Holmes solved this puzzle.'

Then the inspector looks at Sherlock Holmes and asks, 'Holmes, how do you keep on doing it?'

'In this case,' Holmes replies, 'By sitting on the floor for an hour or so smoking a well-stuffed pipe.'